MW01245522

Writing Prompts:

A Collection of Short Stories

Inspired by Imagination

Jan-Carol
Publishing, Inc

"every story needs a book"

Writing Prompts:
A Collection of Short Stories Inspired by Imagination

Published August 2019
Mountain Girl Press
Imprint of Jan Carol Publishing, Inc.

ISBN: 978-1-950895-08-3
Library of Congress Control Number: 2019948263

You may contact the publisher:
Jan-Carol Publishing, Inc.
PO Box 701
Johnson City, TN 37605
publisher@jancarolpublishing.com
jancarolpublishing.com

This book is dedicated to each author who has helped
add to our family at Jan-Carol Publishing, Inc.

Introduction

This book is the result of friendly competition among Jan-Carol Publishing authors. Each flash fiction, or in some cases non-fiction, entry was selected after a brief contest in which authors answered a prompt. The prompts are included in the pages that follow, along with the name of the author for each winning piece.

Table of Contents

Writing Prompt: Write 250 words or less about a character on the Fourth of July. The character can be one you have already or one you create on the fly. Your 250 word story must be FICTION and must include a dandelion AND the American flag. However, your 250 words may NOT include fireworks in any form, because that's too easy!

Winner: Bev Clay Freeman, author of *Silence of the Bones*, *Where Ladies Slippers Grow*, and *Return to Walkers' Mountain*

✽   ✽   ✽

News

R ex Ransom's car passed a line of people who were observing the 4th of July American flags display at the Smoky Mountains' Visitor Center. He exceeded posted speeds and raced toward Dandelion Cove, ignoring the Patriotism of the day. He always had to be first to get the breaking story. Today it was Native American artifacts discovered in the cove, where white settlers were previously thought to be first. But the latest unearthed items might change that belief.

The car slid into a curve as he caught sight of the Channel 5 News Van. Rex floored the accelerator and whisked past them. "Not today, Ms. Sarah. This one is my story." He shook his fist, calling out the window, and passed on double yellow lines.

Torrential rain all day and night had brought creeks out of their banks. The steel bridge where Dandelion Creek joined Roaring Fork was inches from flooding.

As Rex drove onto the wood planking, he saw a wall of water bearing down on the structure. Determined to cross, he continued, but a fifteen-foot wash engulfed the bridge, crushing it like a soda can.

Rex thought, *If only I hadn't gone back for extra camera batteries or stopped for coffee, I'd be there now. How will I get the news on time? It is my story; damn that water!*

Rex struggled to catch his last breath as the car rolled, when it dawned on him, "Tonight, I AM the NEWS."

Writing Prompt: Write 250 words about a summertime experience you've had. Your story must be based in your hometown, must be NON-FICTION, and must be set in either July or August.

Winner: Victoria Fletcher, author of *Fletcher's Fables*, *Fletcher's Fables Too*, and *Cocoa the Basset Hound*

✳ ✳ ✳

Beatle-Mania

My birthday is in July. When I was getting ready to turn 10 years old, my mom asked me what I wanted for my birthday. Before I tell you what I said, I need to give you some background.

I used to stay with my grandparents while my dad taught school and my mom worked at the power company. My uncle still lived at home since he was the baby and only 18 years old. He was the coolest guy I knew. He loved The Beatles' music. Since he did, so did I. He told me they were from Liverpool, England, which was a long way from Damascus. They came to America to be on the Ed Sullivan show. Needless to say, Tom and I were in front of the TV for that. I think my grandparents were glad when that was over. Now, back to my answer.

"Mom, more than anything, I want a Beatles shirt," I said.

"Okay, I will go shopping during my lunch breaks this week," Mom said.

I couldn't wait until after birthday cake and ice cream to open my gift. First, I looked at it, disappointed. Then I became hysterical.

"What is wrong?" my Mom asked.

"Nothing, Mom. I got what I asked for," I said, with tears streaming down my face. It was a shirt with a beetle on it.

Writing Prompt: Write 250 words about the best experience you've ever had while doing a stereotypically mundane activity. For example, the best experience you've ever had getting gas, doing chores, grocery shopping, walking the dog, driving to work, etc. Your 250 words must be NON-FICTION.

Winner: Charlotte S. Snead, author of *A Place to Live*, *Always My Son*, *Winning Cathy*, and *Gracie Goodbye*

✼ ✼ ✼

Childlike Faith

I was on the phone, praying with a friend who called, while battling a severe bout of the flu. I was trying to be upbeat, but I couldn't stand up and instead sank to the floor. My three-year old sank down beside me.

"Are you OK, Mom?"

I whispered that I felt really sick. He ran back to our bedroom, coming back with my Bible in his hand.

He threw it on the floor at my feet, hollering, "Do you see that, debil? We believe every word in this book. Get your filthy hands off my mama!"

Instant healing! The faith of a child! I hugged him, got up, and did a full day's work.

Writing Prompt: Write 250 words about the family of polar bears on an icy landscape in our photo. Did the photographer stumble upon them or track them down? Do you want to include the photographer at all, or are the bears looking at something more interesting? Your 250 words must be FICTION.

Winner: Susanna Connelly Holstein, Anthologies *Easter Lilies* and *These Haunted Hills*

* * *

The Return

I ce hung from his eyebrows and beard as he trudged across the expanse of frozen white and blue. Beside and below him stretched the lake, frozen twenty feet deep. It made for good walking.

He had planned this hike for years, determined to test his endurance against the wilderness that had killed his grandfather and driven his grandmother south, to the beaches of Florida.

There he had grown up, but he had always dreamed of snow, of Northern Lights and polar bears.

All this way, and not a bear to be seen, he thought. He dropped the pack from his back and sank to his haunches. Time to make tea, warm up.

It was a sound as soft as rain. There, so close he could see their breath fog, a mother and her white cubs stood immobile. He froze, one hand on the stove. The mother took a step, nose in the air as she caught his scent. The cubs gamboled behind her, innocently uncaring about this stranger in their land.

The mother came closer, her wild blue eyes locked on his. He didn't blink, didn't twitch, paralyzed by her gaze. A cub ran up and chewed on his mother's leg; she batted him with her huge paw, turned, and lumbered across the ice. The spell was broken.

He watched the bears until they disappeared from sight. Then he made his tea and drank it as he looked back at the way he had come. It was time to go home.

Writing Prompt: Write a 250 word detailed description of an object without explicitly saying what the object is. The goal of this prompt is to practice descriptive language and imagery. If you really want to say what your object is, you may do so ONLY in the last line of your entry.

Winner: Bev Clay Freeman, author of *Silence of the Bones, Where Ladies Slippers Grow,* and *Return to Walkers' Mountain*

✻ ✻ ✻

You Stand Alone

You stand alone, grounded yet surrounded by gold and green. They bow as if to touch the hem of your garment—a wrap, rough in texture, life sustaining, encasing your core, your soul. Concealing rings in time are a memory of your life.

Lift your arms toward heaven's light by day, and shelter those who rest in safety at night. Your grace be honored by all who kneel next to you. You bring forth fruit to those who hunger. Carved by sharp edge, you bleed. Scars heal, leaving deep-cut letters...such a shame. You are old, majestic, and strong but wither at the touch of flames. Your enemy is fire, from which you cannot run.

Spring brings life in sprouts of green and delicate bloom. In summer you cool the world and replenish cleansing oxygen into the air. With autumn your color blushes shades of red and orange. Winter's wind rips through your limbs, leaving you naked. Snow blankets you against the cold. You stand alone.

Writing Prompt: Write a 250 word short story that involves a countdown. Start the story at FIVE and end at ZERO. The story may be either fiction or non-fiction, but it must include SNOW and HIDDEN TREASURE.

Winner: Susanna Connelly Holstein, Anthologies *Easter Lilies* and *These Haunted Hills*

❋ ❋ ❋

Treasure Mountain

Five of them. Out of the settlers huddled at the fort during the Shawnee raid, only five were taken prisoner. Nancy struggled through the deep snow, gripping her son's hand. She, her son, and three men were shoved along the trail by their captors. She tried not to think about why only these few were selected.

Behind her, two Indians struggled with a large iron kettle they'd taken from the fort. She had seen them throwing things into the pot, and now knives, silver, and other items clanked in the kettle. The two men looked like they were having trouble; they soon dropped behind the others. The group stopped, and the two Indians who had dropped behind reappeared, empty-handed. No one mentioned the kettle. They seemed to be arguing about what to do with their captives. Nancy's heart thumped with fear for her little son.

At that moment gunfire burst from the trees. Men rushed from the forest, yelling and whooping. The Shawnee ran swiftly into the gathering dark as soldiers appeared like avenging angels. Tears coursed down Nancy's cheeks. "We are saved! Hallelujah! We are saved!"

This story is based on a Shawnee raid on a small settlement in Pendleton County, West Virginia, in 1758. For years people have searched for the lost kettle and its treasure. At the annual Treasure Mountain Festival, there is a treasure hunt as part of the activities. But of the kettle and its contents, the number of items found to date: zero.

Writing Prompt: Write 250 words about overcoming a fear. It can be fiction or non-fiction, your fear or someone else's. Describe the fear, why it is frightening, and how it was or will be overcome.

Winner: Victoria Fletcher, author of *Fletcher's Fables*, *Fletcher's Fables Too*, and *Cocoa the Basset Hound*

* * *

Acrophobia

Some people are afraid of spiders, snakes, or other animals. Not me. Some people are afraid of dark or closed spaces. Not me. Some people are afraid of doctors and dentists. Not...okay, maybe the dentist a little bit.

My main fear is of heights. I even have trouble getting on the second step of a step stool.

It is a little frustrating not being able to change a light bulb, because I am so short that I can't reach it without the before mentioned second step.

I won't live in a two-story house. I don't even like to visit my friend's house, which has a deck off the second story. Once, she saw me clinging to the wall, and we went back inside. I admire people who can skydive, take chairlifts, stand on overlooks, or just enjoy their deck. I am just not one of them!

There was a brief time that I became comfortable with climbing a step stool. However, after falling head first off the church steps, that was short lived.

Since I am as old as the hills, I doubt the fear will be conquered in this life. I bet it will be cured when I am walking on golden streets way up high. That doesn't scare me a bit.

Writing Prompt: Write 200–250 words about an "Alien Thanksgiving." Is the holiday called the same thing? How did it come about? When does it take place on this foreign planet?

Winner: Victoria Fletcher, author of *Fletcher's Fables*, *Fletcher's Fables Too*, and *Cocoa the Basset Hound*

❅ ❅ ❅

Alien Thanksgiving

On the tiny planet of Zircon, all the beings were blessed to be free from their enemies, the Gargantuans, after years of battles. King Zark announced a day of celebration to show thanks for their freedom. He decided to name the special day Free Feast Day. He invited all 1000 beings of Zircon to attend.

On the day of the feast, all the beings came with food to share, and the day was enjoyed by all. The tiny beings sang to the adults. The king arranged rides to the nearby galaxy, Xavier, and back. They used the planet's moons, which were perfect diamond shapes, to play baseball, using their jet-ski boots to run bases.

It was a great day of fun, food, and fellowship. During the feast the king asked each being to share why they were thankful. I think tiny Zubidia said it best. She said, "I am thankful for freedom, my family and friends, and, most of all, for having a God of the Universe watching over me.

At the end of the day, King Zark told the Zirconias that he was declaring Free Feast Day to be an annual event. "We will hold it on the 20th of Zeldathan to commemorate the day we became free." All the beings of Zircon cheered.

Writing Prompt: Write 200–250 words about a winter love affair. This story can be true or fictional, but it MUST include snow, like all truly great winter love stories do.

Winner: Willie Dalton, author of *Three Witches in a Small Town* and *The Dark Side of the Woods*

* * *

A Love Like Winter

I had missed him. I hadn't seen his face since spring, but that's how it went every year. When the air started to chill and the sky started to gray, that's when he called. And when the snow began to melt and flowers started to bloom, we would inevitably part ways, even though neither of us really wanted to. He was my winter lover and the only thing that warmed my cold heart in those dreary days.

We met at our spot, which was just off the highway, at the head of a hiking trail that led through a tunnel. We weren't supposed to be there this late, but no one would be coming to close the gate in this weather. The roads were icy, and we were crazy to be out in it ourselves, but seeing each other was worth it. He took my arm and smiled at me, reminding me of everything I had been missing for so many months.

17

We walked arm in arm through the glittering snow, with the streetlamps casting a dreamlike glow across the ground and our faces. And that's what it was really—a dream that lasted from December to March. He kissed me there in the cold, with snowflakes in our hair, and I knew there was no other love like my winter love.

Writing Prompt: Write 200–250 words about the New Year. What are your goals? What steps have you taken to reach them? What adventures are you planning?

Winner: Stacey Lynn Schlegl, author of *Little Frog*; *Tiny Learns to Listen*; and *MerMountain*

❊ ❊ ❊

Finding Peace One Minute at a Time

My goal for 2018 is to shed the weight of my past and live for my future. Many years ago—twenty-three years, two months, and twenty-six days, to be exact—I was attacked in my very dorm room in college. Despite this tragedy, I went on with my life to finish college at the top of my class, to have four beautiful girls, and to have twenty-two years of marriage. I fooled myself in believing I was a survivor and that I had overcome. I was one of the strong ones. However, I was not one of the strong ones. I tricked myself into believing I was. I got my strength from food. I deserved that donut. I needed that extra helping of spaghetti. I went from 130 pounds to 300 pounds.

This year, 2018, I decided to take my life back and find inner peace. On January 1, I worked out twenty minutes, and every day since, I have added one minute to my workout. Today I reached forty-eight minutes. In my mind it is forty-eight minutes that I have taken back from the clutches of darkness in which time stood still without me realizing it. I was slowly dying and unaware of my slow departure. It will not be easy to find my peace after I am back under one hundred and seventy pounds of pain, but I know that I have no choice. I will not let my past define me. I will not let evil take my future away. My girls need a mom to help them pick out wedding dresses, to hold and rock their children, and to love them. This is a battle I will win by losing.

Writing Prompt: Write 200–250 words about the last stranger you took notice of for some reason. Who was the last random person to catch your eye? What did they look like? Where do you think they were headed? Could you create a story around them?

Winner: Linda Hudson Hoagland, author of *The Lindsay Harris Murder Mystery Series*; *Onward & Upward*; *Missing Sammy*; and *The Best Darn Secret*

* * *

Homeless

Left Turn Linda should be my new name because of my insatiable desire to drive off in the wrong direction. I did exactly that when I went in search of the Harvest Table, where I could set up and sell my books.

Having finally found the establishment, I exited my car and went in search of the person I needed to talk with to get myself set up and ready to sell.

I started to walk to the front of the building, and I spotted a walking, raggedy-clothed man, who was disheveled to the point of needing a good scrubbing. He was no more than five-two, with long, straggly gray hair and a dirty beard and mustache. He had tied cloth bags, which appeared to be empty and waiting to be filled with whatever, from his shoulders.

Initially I was frightened of this little man, but when he said "hello" in a bright, cheerful tone, my first impression changed.

He appeared to be homeless but not unhappy. He didn't ask me for anything, for which I was relieved because that would have caused my opinion of him to be drastically different.

I believed he was on his way to collect cans and other paraphernalia that would earn him some eating or drinking money.

If I hadn't been running late for my commitment to set up and sell my books, I would have loved to have talked with him. I might have contributed some funds to help him survive.

Writing Prompt: Write 200–250 words about an unusual Valentine's Day love story. Do NOT include flowers, chocolates, cards, or typical V-Day gifts, such as stuffed animals. Create a love story around something more unique! Keep in mind that, while your submission can feature two people 'in love,' love stories don't always have to be between significant others or even between humans!

Winner: Rosie Hartwig-Benson, author of *Petals of Distinction*

❋ ❋ ❋

Whispers of Love

The first time we met was in the tranquility of a mountainside park. A majestic sunrise peeked over the horizon. A warm breeze drifted over the flowing river bank. I inhaled deeply. My senses elevated with the divine perfume of pure, fresh air. Daily concerns dissipated.

A well-worn hiking path had unexpected turns, with winding brick pavers under tall pines. A piercing vocalization surrounded me. A Renaissance-inspired water fountain stood stately in the center of the seven acres. Water cascaded gently from the three-tiered fountain while I listened to his endearing whistles. His song resonated with vibrancy.

My heart skipped a beat when I finally caught a glimpse of him. It was love at first sight. He appeared to be playing hide and seek while peering through the leaves of the nearby shrub. The striking jewel was wearing a red coat. It was a stunning crimson that I couldn't take my eyes off of. He had a distinctive crest on his head and a black mask on his face. His sweet melody transported my mind and body into a blissful and meditative state.

Nature's healing wonders of awe-inspiring sights and soothing sounds made for an enchanted setting for this Valentine love story to unfold. A wrought iron bench provided a place for us to rest, with him perched on the back bar. I embraced the gift of being alive. A reservoir of peace and love encased me in harmony.

Writing Prompt: Use 200–250 words to describe the best book you've ever read. However, do NOT give that book a name. You can use character names if you feel the need to, but try to describe the story without blatantly telling your readers what it is!

Winner: Linda Hudson Hoagland, author of *The Lindsay Harris Murder Mystery Series*; *Onward & Upward*; *Missing Sammy*; and *The Best Darn Secret*

✳ ✳ ✳

The Right Thing

My lawyer daddy was raising my brother and me in Alabama during the depression. Things were different then because not all people were treated the same. If your skin was darker, you weren't treated like the white folks.

We had playmates with that darker skin, and the only thing I could see that was different about them was their skin color. My friends weren't allowed to go to the same school I went to, and sometimes they didn't go at all.

My daddy, the lawyer, decided to take a case defending a man of color. That seemed to be a mistake as far as our neighbors were concerned. It was thought that the black man shouldn't be defended; instead, they believed he should be taken out to the nearest tall tree and hung by the neck until dead.

My daddy said the black man didn't rape the white girl, and it was my daddy's job to prove that the accused black man was innocent.

People were really angry with my daddy and decided the best way to get back at him was to kill me and my brother.

One of the people with the darker skin saved my brother and me from being murdered by a crazy man.

Even though things did not work out the way my daddy wanted them to, he felt he had done the right thing.

Writing Prompt: Go over to your bookshelf, close your eyes, and pick up the first book you touch. Open the book to a random page, read the first full sentence on that page, and use it as the inspiration for a story or scene. Please include the original line at the beginning or end of your response, and stay within the 200–250 word limit!

Winner: April Ford Hensley

✲ ✲ ✲

The Happiest Day

"It could only have happened to you," the chef snapped, almost dancing with anger.

"Look at me when I'm talking to you."

I lifted my eyes and wiped my hands nervously on my apron. Chef Marconi had his beefy hands clenched at his sides. I tried hard to keep a straight face, but when I noticed his eyes were still running, I felt my bottom lip quiver.

"Do you think this is funny, Maria?" He dabbed his eyes with a napkin. "Those apple pies were the dessert of the day. We have a dining room full of people begging for water. The Smith's rehearsal dinner is ruined."

I quickly covered my face and turned away, my shoulders shaking with laughter. The big Italian, thinking I was overcome with emotion, patted me awkwardly on the shoulder.

"There, there. I'm sorry I yelled at you. Mistakes happen with new employees. From now on, though, let's not mix up the cinnamon with the chili powder. Capiche?"

I nodded silently. "Take a little break, and then get rid of those disgusting pies."

Marconi shuffled out to the dining room to apologize again. I scurried over to peer through the gap in the swinging door.

There sat my ex-fiancé and my ex-best friend. Jeremy and Brittany were fanning their faces while clutching glasses of water, as were both of their families. Today ended up being the happiest day of my life after all.

First sentence from *The Mystery of the Ghostly Galleon* by Kathryn Kenny.

Writing Prompt: Write 250 words about a place where it is always winter, a place where the residents haven't seen the ground under the snow in 50 years. Then, make all the snow melt. What's under it? What do people do?

Winner: Teresa Jewell, author of *My Bucket's Got a Hole in It*

* * *

The Glacier

The glacier had been there long before any historical mapping. As a scientist I had studied its recession for years, but now, since the seasons have changed, it is gone. Something just kept me coming back here. The rocks and dirt are exposed now, and the ice and snow are almost gone. The Inuit tribe gave me permission to invite my fellow scientists. The research group camped on the outcrop and immediately started mineral samples. In the first samples, we found gold and precious and semiprecious stones. But the best thing uncovered under the last bit of snow was a perfectly preserved mummy.

The mummy was believed to be a hunter that fell into a crevasse and broke his leg during a storm. We took DNA samples from the specimen and dated him back to 175,000 years. The strangest thing was a unique "Y" chromosome he carried. Our scientific team searched the data banks for a match. One man matched the "Y" chromosome. I was the only match in the whole modern world.

I now wear the talisman the mummy carried. After all, this was a family heirloom. The mummy rests now at the Smithsonian in Washington, DC.

Because of this incredible discovery, this desolate place will now be studied for years and will be excavated for studying early man and the stories left behind in the rock and soil. All the gold unearthed will go to the tribe, and the rest we will be utilized to supplement the dig.

Writing Prompt: Write 200–250 words about the wildest, most unique 'egg hunt' you can imagine. The crazier the better! Who's involved? Where does the hunt take place? Is it for Easter or another holiday? Are there prizes?

Winner: Stacey Lynn Schlegl, author of *Little Frog*; *Tiny Learns to Listen*; and *MerMountain*

✲ ✲ ✲

Have a Hoppy Halloween

M om!" Tiffany rolled her eyes. "It's Halloween. I can't believe you would embarrass me like this."

"There is nothing wrong with me dressing as the Easter Bunny and giving out eggs with candy inside—recycling at its finest."

"What if my friends see you? What if Drew finds out? He will never ask me to the dance!"

The doorbell rang. Lisa hopped over. Two pirates stood and held their bags open.

Lisa gave them eggs and sang, "HOPPY Halloween!" She hopped back to her daughter. "I thought it was a cute idea. You're always telling me to wear more makeup. I am wearing plenty of mascara and lipstick."

Tiffany rolled her eyes. "I meant mascara on your eyes, not on your cheeks as whiskers, and I meant lipstick on your lips, not your NOSE!"

"I guess you should've been clearer." Lisa hopped back over to answer the bell.

In the doorway stood two guys who were dressed as football players. She plopped two eggs into their pillowcases and said, "Could that be Drew Smith and Bill Jones?"

"Hi, Mrs. C." Drew smiled. "I promise to go home and do my science homework."

Tiffany came to the door with an embarrassed look.

Lisa Cunningham smiled and said, "Open your eggs."

Drew and Bill opened their eggs, and inside was a 'No Homework Pass.'

"Your mom is the best teacher ever!" Drew grinned.

Bill poked Drew. "Ask her."

Drew blushed and asked, "Tiffany, do you have a date to the dance yet?"

Writing Prompt: Write 200–250 words about your DREAM SUMMER VACATION. Now, when we say dream, we mean go all out. Nothing can stop you. Make it as realistic or fantasy inspired as you like!

Winner: Bev Clay Freeman, author of *Silence of the Bones*, *Where Ladies Slippers Grow*, and *Return to Walkers' Mountain*

❋ ❋ ❋

If

You look at the numbers on the TV screen, shake your head, and look again. "No way!"

You pick up a pen and rewrite the numbers. "I got 'em all! Oh shit!"

The next day, you listen to the news; "One winner!" was all you heard. "And I'm it!"

Two weeks later you're standing on an island beach, alone. Your island—fifty three acres of subtropical beauty, one beach house, no roads, protected harbor with your seventy foot yacht, and no one to tell you what to do.

"I must be dreaming." You kick a shell with your bare foot. "Ouch!" Not dreaming, are you?

The temperature is a breezy seventy-two degrees. You feel hunger nagging, so you return to your dwelling. Up the stairs, onto natural wood flooring of your covered deck, through the open door, and into the dining area. Your 360-degree view offers distant mountains, miles of aquamarine water, and sailboats in vibrant colors, which dot the surface like tiny floating birds.

You take a bowl of fresh fruit, a cheese tray with crackers, and a bottle of your favorite wine to the hammock. Each swing in the breeze brings you close enough to the rail to pick up another bite of lunch. Who needs a glass? You sip the wine from the bottle, the way you've always wanted to. No guilt, no rules—just you, your imagination, and your laptop. Today you will finish your fifth novel. Janie patiently waits for another best seller.

Writing Prompt: Write 200–300 word story that involves confusion over homonyms (words that have the same spelling but different meanings) or homophones (words that sound the same but are spelled differently). Need help? A quick Google search will give you a long list of both!

Winner: Stacey Lynn Schlegl, author of *Little Frog; Tiny Learns to Listen;* and *MerMountain*

* * *

What a Zoo!

D uck!"
Ben ducked and put his hands over his head.

"No, silly! There is a duck!" Betsy laughed, pointing too a duck flying overhead.

"You no you really shouldn't scare me like that."

"Sorry." She chewed her gum.

"You no Mom says knot two chew the inside of you're mouth like that. Don't let her sea ewe dew that. She says it will ruin you're gums," Ben warned.

"Really? Does Mom no you still pick you're nose?"

"What I due with my nose is my own business...such a big boar."

"I am not a bore! That is plane rude." Betsy put her hands on her hips.

Ben rolled his iii. "Know, their is a boar over there. Its really big."

"I am thinking we need to keep moving. We are supposed to meat Mom."

"I am fifteen. I don't need to check-in."

"Well, I due. I am only ten."

"Yak!" Ben shouted.

"We are at the ZOO. Their are yaks," Betsy said with sarcasm. Her foot slipped, and she landed smack on her butt in a smelly mess.

"No, I meant they're is yak on the ground," Ben chuckled. "I think mom isn't going to bee two concerned with me picking my nose when ewe are covered in puke."

Betsy was horrified.

Ben switched the bare's nose he was wearing to a pig's nose and made an oinking noise. "You stink!"

"I might stink, but mom is write behind ewe."

Ben stumbled and fell.

"I thought I told ewe know more silly costume noses at you're age. And, Betsy, how in the world did ewe fall into vomit??!"

They're mom stepped backwards with her hand on her nose. "Oh crap!"

"Mom!" Both kids reprimanded.

There mom pointed. Sure enough, Ben had fallen into crap. WHAT A ZOO!

Writing Prompt: For this prompt, simply answer the question below: What if you could travel though time? Explain your adventure in 200–250 words.

Winner: Linda Hudson Hoagland, author of *The Lindsay Harris Murder Mystery Series*; *Onward & Upward*; *Missing Sammy*; and *The Best Darn Secret*

❋ ❋ ❋

Golden Years

Time travel would take me twenty to thirty years ahead so I could watch my sons mature into old gentlemen, soaking in the good that life has to offer until the very end of their days.

Both sons endured a difficult youth; one son was hit by a car when he was a teenager, in which he sustained a devastating skull fracture, a broken leg, and many cuts and abrasions, while the other son had to survive the neglect that was dealt to him when his mother and stepfather had to tend to the needs of his seriously damaged brother.

I want to gaze into the future so I can see how old age has treated my boys, because I believe they have earned their share of the golden years.

It has been a struggle for me to arrive at this point in my life. I lived through two bad marriages before I finally got the marriage thing right with my third husband. Number three, Sonny, lasted for twenty-five years, until his death.

I had to care for my mother during her declining years, at which time she was losing her mental capacity.

While married to Sonny, I cared for him as he survived back surgeries, heart surgeries, diabetes, and his final heart attack. But I can't complain.

I played the hand I was dealt, and I am content with my life at this point. I hope my boys feel that way when they each reach my age and beyond.

Writing Prompt: As a child, did you always plan to be an author? Describe in 200–250 words the first moment you wrote out a story and thought, *Wow, I can really do this.* Give JCP and your fellow authors some insight on how writing became your passion!

Winner: Elizabeth Buttke, author of *Deep in the Holler: Appalachian Tales* and *Tell Me a Story: Appalachian Tales*

* * *

Once Upon a Dream

As a child, and as an adult, I never fathomed being an author one day. From an early age, I always loved a good story, and I loved to hear one told. In grade school English, at some point you are asked to write paragraphs, then short stories. This taught me that I could write down all of the thoughts and stories that went around in my head daily.

A writer sees a story in almost everything—a person, place, or memory. Things long forgotten come alive to you, like when you see a deserted home-place or an old person sitting outside a country store. You want to know their stories. I started writing little stories by age eleven, and later I wrote poems. All through the years, if it moved something deep in me, I wrote it down. It took someone finding out I had done this and encouraging me before I took a leap and submitted some of my stories. Books had been my dear friends for many years, and that's all I wanted my book to be to someone.

Now, as an author, I cherish a good book more than ever, and I respect the author even more. The biggest rewards I have gotten from writing have been moments when people call and cry because a certain story moved them or brought back a memory and made them laugh. Only then do I feel like a writer.

Writing Prompt: Write 200–250 words about two people seeing each other for the first time. The only requirement? Your story must either START OR END with the word "Hello."

Winner: Teresa Stutso Jewell, author of *My Bucket's Got a Hole in It*

* * *

Hello at Last

Have you ever been in a crowded room, not knowing anybody, and then suddenly you feel someone staring at you, and you can feel their eyes and feel the draw? I went to my cousin's wedding; I felt obligated to since we had grown up together. Having a plane trip to Florida, and having it paid for, was certainly another incentive for going. The wedding was beautiful and on the beach, and then the reception was outside on a hotel's ocean plaza. The band was playing all of my favorite songs, and I couldn't help but move to the beat. I guess I did draw attention, being almost six feet tall and wearing a very low-cut yellow sundress. My hair was pulled back, but it was left down in the back, showing off my tan. I was the tallest and probably the youngest unmarried woman there.

Everywhere I turned, I felt him looking at me. I would casually look his way, and he would smile, and I smiled back, but then I would turn away and act like I didn't notice "Mr. tall, dark, and

41

handsome." I had to find something to drink, so I tried to get to the bar. Just when I was ready to order, he was standing beside me with two glasses of Champagne. I looked up at him, and he smiled. Taking a second, I took the glass from his hand. I sipped slowly, still looking into his blue eyes and seeing my reflection in them. He finally said, "Hello."

Writing Prompt: You (or a character) have been enjoying a leisurely walk down a familiar wooded path for an hour when you suddenly realize that you no longer know where you are. Trusting that your current path will lead you back home—because it logically should—you turn around. In 250 words or less, explain where the path actually leads you and the things that you encounter.

Winner: Bev Clay Freeman, author of *Silence of the Bones*, *Where Ladies Slippers Grow*, and *Return to Walkers' Mountain*

✳ ✳ ✳

Out

L eaves show their undersides.
"I've always heard that means rain. At least it's cooler with the breeze."

She walks the same trail every day. Solitude is therapy.

"The breeze is steady now. Maybe I should turn back."

She stops, looking behind her. Things appear to be different.

"I followed the creek. Where's the rocky stream that's lined with mountain laurel? There's just this field of Black-eyed Susan."

Billowy clouds move slowly overhead.

"Which way is home? I don't remember this...wait, it's the place we flew kites as children. And there's Adam. But he's...it can't be. And there's Granny."

She turns again. The sky darkens. Storm clouds block the sun.

"Where'd they go?"

She spins in circles. Snow gathers around her feet. Bare arms hug her chest.

"Where's my coat? I'm so cold."

There are no tracks.

"That house...I see a light."

She walks closer; the house moves away. She sees footprints leading toward her but none behind.

"Where was I going?"

She turns to continue her walk, now on cobblestone streets. Colorful, small shops line both sides. People wave. A man bids her good day and tips his hat.

"Mr. O, how—?"

The street is suddenly dark; pain streaks through her body.

She shields her eyes against the bright sun, which is hot on her skin. Beyond the light, eyes stare down on her, faces hidden behind masks!

"Welcome back. That was quite a blow you got from that branch. Are you ready to stay for a while?"

About the Authors

Rosie Hartwig-Benson is a spirit-filled survivor and author of *Petals of Distinction*. She is a native of Minnesota, a devoted mother, nature enthusiast, photographer, and designer.

Elizabeth Hardin Buttke is the author of *Deep in the Holler* and *Tell Me a Story*. She holds a diploma in Medical Records and is a former substitute teacher. She still resides on her mother's home-place where she grew up. She spends her spare time writing, painting, and enjoying her two grandkids.

Victoria Fletcher was a former teacher and secretary/ministry assistant at First Baptist Church in Damascus, Virginia. She retired in 2018 to pursue her publishing business, Hoot Books Publishing, which is located at the Virginia Highlands Small Business Incubator in Abingdon, VA. Currently, she has written 21 books.

Bev Freeman resides with her family in Unicoi County, the foothills of the Appalachian Mountains. The author of a Mystery Trilogy, she also enjoys art and is presently learning watercolor painting. Bev's fourth mystery novel is in the works with the hope of publishing in 2020.

April Hensley resides in the peaceful mountains of East Tennessee with her husband and beloved fur-babies. She is the author of three published short stories, "Hallelujah Homecoming," "Forever," and "Riverview Road" writing as Maggie Thomas. April has also published online and is a regular contributor to *Voice Magazine for Women*.

Linda Hudson Hoagland is the author of fiction, nonfiction, short stories, poetry, and stage plays. Hoagland has won numerous awards for her work, including first place for the Pearl S. Buck Award for Social Change and the Sherwood Anderson Short Story Contest. Her work has appeared in many anthologies and literary magazines.

Teresa Stutso Jewell teaches English, Literature, and Appalachian Studies at Southwest Virginia Community College. She writes and sings bluegrass music with her husband's band. Jewell is an artist, and uses painting and sculpting to keep her fear of boredom at bay. She writes poetry, music, and short stories.

Stacey Schlegl is a scientist/geneticist and mother of four girls. She enjoys writing science books for children to encourage reading. Schlegl also writes juvenile fiction with her oldest daughter. Schlegl has written over 22 novels. Her professional blog is MyMillionDollarIdeas.com, on which she posts toy, game, and marketing ideas.

Charlotte S. Snead published her first book at age 69. Now 76, has eight published books. When her first publisher went out of business, Snead won Jan-Carol Publishing's Believe and Achieve award, and they contracted her for all five books in her *Hope House Girls* series. Snead has also published one book with Van Rye Publishing.

**Jan-Carol
Publishing, Inc**

"every story needs a book"

www.JANCAROLPUBLISHING.com

CPSIA information can be obtained
at www.ICGtesting.com
Printed in the USA
LVHW091600070222
710472LV00005B/334